LET'S TAKE A WALK IN THE

by Karen O'Connor
and Deborah Crowdy
illustrated by Lois Axeman

ELGIN, ILLINOIS 60120

Distributed by Childrens Press, 1224 West Van Buren Street,
Chicago, Illinois 60607.

Library of Congress Cataloging in Publication Data

O'Connor, Karen.
Let's take a walk in the city.

(Five senses walk series)
Summary: Tony uses his five senses to enjoy a walk in the city with his mother.
[1. Senses and sensation—Fiction. 2. City and town life—Fiction] I. Crowdy, Deborah, 1953-
II. Axeman, Lois, ill. III. Title. IV. Series.
PZ7.T4223Le 1986 [E] 86-20746
ISBN 0-89565-355-9

1 2 3 4 5 6 7 8 9 10 11 12 R 93 92 91 90 89 88 87 86

LET'S TAKE A WALK IN THE CITY

13284
SUNSHINE
FROM

"We're here," Tony says. "What a big place!" He looks down the busy street at the tall, tall buildings.

Everywhere there are people. . .
crowds of people. . .hurrying people.
A big, black limousine pulls up at the

curb. Yellow taxis line up in a row, as if playing, "Follow-the-Leader." Tony likes the hurry-scurry all around him.

Looking up, he sees a glassy, skyway
bridge, crossing high over the cars. . .

a pointy church steeple. . .a glittering movie sign. . .and the glow of traffic lights.

Tony and his mom stop before a big store window.

"Look, Tony! It's Snow White and the Seven Dwarfs."

Tony laughs as Dopey trips over his own feet!

"Here, Mom, look! A window full of toys!" says Tony, pressing his nose against the icy windowpane. As Tony watches a walking robot, the snowfall

becomes heavier. The soft snowflakes touch Tony's cheeks.

"We came at just the right time to buy your mittens and boots," says Mom.

The mittens feel soft and fluffy—
just right for a snowy day!

The boots feel warm and furry.

"Wow!" says Tony. "These are just right. Can I wear them?"

"Sure," says Mom.

As they leave the store, Tony hears music. He slips his hand into his pocket and touches a shiny quarter. He hears the clink as he throws the coin into the kettle.

Outside, Tony hears the city sounds—honks, beeps, sirens, a policeman's whistle.

Sounds are everywhere—all around, above and below. A subway rumbles under Tony's feet. High above, a jet comes in to land.

The fumes from the cars and buses
make Tony want to cough!

But he likes the sweet, spicy smell of a small candle shop.

Tony likes the smells of many good things in the city—spaghetti simmering . . . hot dogs broiling.

He especially likes the smells of the bakery. . .

and the yummy smells from a small candy shop.

"I'm hungry," says Tony. "Isn't it time to eat?"

"Yes," says Mom. "And I know just the place. What's your favorite food?"

"Pizza!" Tony says.

CANDIES

Tony likes the taste of the hot pizza,

the cold milk,

and the even colder ice cream.

When Tony and his mom go outside, they hear an old gold clock above a jewelry store chime. Ding! Ding! Ding! Ding! Ding!

"Time to go," says Tony's mom. "It's getting late!"

They hurry toward the bus stop and hear the squeal of brakes as the bus slows down.

BUS
STOP

Tony looks out the window of the bus at all the lights. He thinks about his day in the city.

"Can we come again soon, Mom?" he asks.